Misty the Abandoned Kitten

Holly Webb

Illustrated by Sophy Williams

Stripes

For Tabitha

For more information about Holly Webb visit:
www.holly-webb.com

STRIPES PUBLISHING
An imprint of Little Tiger Press
1 The Coda Centre, 189 Munster Road,
London SW6 6AW

A paperback original
First published in Great Britain in 2010

Text copyright © Holly Webb, 2010
Illustrations copyright © Sophy Williams, 2010

ISBN: 978-1-84715-126-1

A CIP catalogue record for this book is available
from the British Library.

Printed and bound in the UK.

10 9 8 7 6

Chapter One

Amy yawned and rolled over to go back to sleep. But then she stopped halfway and bounced up in bed. It was her birthday! Was it too early to go and wake up Mum and Dad? Amy grabbed her watch off the bedside table. Half-past six. Surely that was late enough, on a birthday?

Shivering slightly in the chill

morning, she threw on her dressing gown, and hurried along the landing to her parents' room.

"Oh! Amy... Happy Birthday..." Her dad yawned hugely. "Is it as early as it feels?"

"It's already half-past six," Amy replied. "Can't we get up? Please, Mum?"

Her mum was already starting to climb out of bed. "You'd better go and get dressed."

"OK!" Amy grinned. She dashed back to her room and started to put on her school uniform, sighing a little. It was so unfair to have to go to school on her birthday. Still, as she was up early, at least Mum might let her open some of her presents...

Amy ran down the stairs eagerly and

burst into the kitchen.

"Oh, wow!" she said, as she sat down at the table in front of a pile of birthday presents. She smiled as she saw that her mum had draped fairy lights round the window. "That looks fab!"

"Well, since you've got to go to school, I thought I'd try and make breakfast special." Amy's mum put a chocolate croissant in front of her.

Just then, Dad came into the kitchen. "I hope there's one for me too," he said, giving Amy a hug. "Happy Birthday!"

"Go on, open your presents," her mum said, smiling.

Amy reached out for the nearest parcel, which was enticingly squashy.

"Oh, it's lovely. Gran's so clever!" she said, as she tore off the paper and shook out a purple hoodie top, with a pink satin cat stitched on to the back, and glittery stars all around.

Her mum smiled. "I told her anything with a cat on it."

When Amy had finally unwrapped all her presents, her dad shook his head. "Do you know, anyone would think you liked cats!" he remarked, staring at the cat T-shirt, cat lunch box, kitten pencil case, and the gorgeous toy Persian cat on Amy's lap. Her mum and dad knew how much she loved cats. But they just didn't think she was old enough to have one as a pet, however much she begged.

"Come on, we need to get to school," Mum pointed out. "I've arranged for you to go for tea at Lily's today, Amy."

Amy looked up in surprise. It was the first she'd heard about this.

Her dad winked. "I need a bit of extra time to sort out your surprise present from us. Didn't you notice we haven't given you anything yet? It'll be waiting for you when you get home."

"Oh!" Amy beamed at him. That sounded really exciting…

"Do you think the surprise could be a kitten?" Amy asked Lily, for about the fifteenth time that day. The girls had finished their tea and had gone up to Lily's room to chat.

Her best friend sighed. "I *still* don't know! Did it sound like they'd changed their minds the last time you asked?"

Amy shook her head. "Mum said I wasn't old enough to look after a pet properly. I told her you do!"

Lily smiled and stroked Stella, her big tabby cat, who was curled up on the duvet between them. "I was lucky. Mum loves cats. I didn't have to beg!"

"Dad could have needed the time to go and fetch a kitten." Amy was thinking aloud. "I can't think of anything else it would be. Oh, I just don't know!" She leaned down so she was nose to nose with Stella, who stared back at her sleepily. "I wish you could tell me. Am I getting a kitten at last?"

Stella yawned, showing all her teeth.
"Hmmm. I'm not sure what that means." Amy sighed. "Oh! Is that the doorbell?" she exclaimed, scrambling to her feet.

Lily frowned. "It's rude to be so happy about going home!" She laughed at Amy's suddenly worried face. "I'm only teasing! Go! Go on! I've got all my fingers crossed for you! Call and tell me if it *is* a kitten!"

A few streets away, a little black kitten was sitting in a cardboard carrier, mewing sadly. She didn't like it in here, and things didn't smell right. She wanted to go back to her lovely home.

"Sshh, sshh, Jet." There was a scuffling noise at the top of the box, and the kitten looked up nervously. "Let's get you out, little one."

The kitten pressed herself into the corner as the dark box opened up. Then she gave a squeak of relief. There was her owner!

Mrs Jones reached in and gently lifted out the little cat. She lowered herself down into an armchair and the kitten curled up on her lap.

"Can we play with Jet, Gran?" Two children had followed Mrs Jones into the room. "Please!" the little girl squealed.

"Millie, calm down!" Mrs Jones said firmly. "You'll scare her."

The kitten looked up at the children, both reaching out for her, and squirmed into Mrs Jones's cardigan.

"I just want to stroke her," the little boy begged.

"I'm sorry, Dan. I know you both want to say hello, but she's only just arrived, and she's not really used to being with children. She'll soon settle in, I'm sure, and then you can play with her all you want."

"Don't bother Gran, you two. You know she needs to rest and get better." The children's mother was standing in the doorway now. "Do you want a cup of tea or anything, Mum?"

"No, no, Sarah, thank you. I'm just going to sit here with Jet to keep me company."

"OK. Come on, you two. Don't forget to shut the door – you know we need to keep Jet in here for the next few days."

The children ran off after their mum, and the kitten relaxed. This place wasn't home, but at least Mrs Jones was here.

"Oh dear, it's a big change, isn't it?" The old lady tickled her under the chin. "Still, Sarah's right. I'm better off here where she can keep an eye on me."

But Jet wasn't listening. She'd tensed up again, the fur on her tiny black tail bristling. Millie and Dan hadn't shut the door properly after all, and there was another cat here. A big Siamese staring at her with round blue eyes. She mewed anxiously. Did this house already belong to another cat?

Mrs Jones looked over at the cat. "Oh, there's Charlie. Don't worry, Jet. He's friendly; Sarah told me he'd be no trouble. No trouble at all."

"Come out into the garden!" Amy's dad held open the back door, an excited expression on his face.

"The present is outside?" Amy asked doubtfully. Why would a kitten be outside? She stepped out, and looked round at her parents, who were beaming at her.

"Look at the tree!" Dad pointed up at the big chestnut tree at the end of the garden.

"Oh! A tree house!" Amy said, sounding rather surprised.

"Don't you like it?" Her dad's voice was suddenly anxious.

"Yes, I do, I love it." Amy hugged him. It was true − she had always wanted a little private hideaway of her own. It was just that it wasn't a kitten...

"Why don't you go and explore?" said Mum.

Amy ran down the garden and climbed the wooden ladder that her dad had fastened on to the tree trunk.

The tree house smelled lovely, of new wood. Amy looked round it delightedly. There was a big purple beanbag to sit on, and on a tiny wooden table by the square window was a birthday cake, with pink icing.

Amy leaned out of the door, and smiled down at her parents. "It's a brilliant present. Thank you!"

"We'll cut the cake in about half an hour, OK?" said Mum, smiling.

Amy sat down on the beanbag, and sighed. She loved the tree house – but at the same time, she was secretly a little disappointed. "I should have known it wouldn't be a kitten," she whispered to herself. "It was just that I was really hoping…"

Chapter Two

On Saturday it was Amy's birthday party. She and Lily and a couple of other friends from school were going to the cinema, and then to her favourite café for tea. She was really looking forward to it – but every so often something would remind her about kittens and she'd feel sad again.

"I can never decide whether to have sweet or salty popcorn," said Lily, as she and Amy walked over to the food counter. "Or do you want to share some pick 'n' mix instead? Amy…?" She turned to her friend. "Are you OK? You seem a bit quiet," she whispered. "Is it about your present?"

Amy nodded. "My tree house is really cool. I can't wait for you to see it." She sighed. "Maybe they'll change their minds about me getting a cat in time for my next birthday."

Lily gave her a hug. "You can come and borrow Stella any time."

Amy smiled at her gratefully, but it wasn't the same as a kitten of her own.

Mrs Jones's daughter, Sarah, had promised her that Charlie would be fine with having another cat in the house. She was really worried about her mum, who'd had a couple of bad falls, and she wanted to be able to look after her. And that meant her kitten, too. But Sarah just hadn't realized how jealous Charlie would be.

"Come on! Auntie Grace says she's made a cake!" The children were struggling into their coats, and Sarah was trying to hurry everyone up. It was Sunday, and all the family were going over to visit Mrs Jones's other daughter.

Jet heard the front door bang, Mrs Jones's stick tapping as she went down the front step and then the noise of the children growing fainter as they walked down the path. They were all going out! Jet shivered. She was hiding under a bookshelf in the living room. It was very low to the ground and she'd discovered that Charlie couldn't chase her under there, as he was too big. It wasn't a very nice place to stay – it was dusty and she had to lie flat to fit – but at least it was safe.

Now that she was allowed out of the living room and into the rest of the house, Jet spent almost the whole time hiding from Charlie. He kept pouncing on her, and he was a lot bigger than she was. They had been sharing the house properly for almost a week now, and he hadn't got any better. He kept stealing her food, too, so she was hungry all the time. But he was sneaky enough only to do it when no one was looking. If the family were there he would just glare at her until she felt too scared to eat and slunk away from her bowl.

Jet couldn't see him now, though. Perhaps he'd gone out of the cat flap into the garden? Nervously, she edged only her whiskers out of her hiding place and waited. She risked a paw out, then another, then squirmed forwards, her heart racing. No, he wasn't there. She was safe.

She was terribly hungry, though. Charlie had chased her away from her breakfast that morning, and she really wanted to go to the kitchen and see if he'd left anything. With her whiskers trembling and her tail fluffed up, the kitten crept out into the hallway, and dashed to the kitchen door, where she did another careful search. She couldn't see him anywhere. And there was some food left! Gratefully, she scampered over to her bowl, and started to gulp down the cat biscuits.

Behind her, on one of the kitchen chairs, hidden by the plastic tablecloth, a long chocolate-brown tail began to twitch slowly back and forth.

Jet was so absorbed in wolfing what was left of her breakfast that she didn't hear the thud as Charlie's paws hit the floor. But some sense of danger made her whiskers prickle, and she turned round just as he flung himself at her. She shot away, scooting across the kitchen floor and making a dive for the cat flap. She batted at it desperately with her nose and scrambled through, racing across the garden to hide under a bush.

Huddled against the damp leaves, she watched the cat flap swing a couple of times. Charlie wasn't following her. Probably because he was eating the rest of her breakfast, Jet thought miserably.

What should she do? She hadn't explored the garden much until now –

she'd always stayed close to Mrs Jones, or hidden herself somewhere in the house. Jet poked her nose out from under the bush, sniffing the crisp morning air. It was chilly – too chilly to sit still. But she didn't want to go back inside, not with Charlie about. Instead, she set off down the garden, sniffing at the bird seed that had fallen out of the bird feeders, and cautiously inspecting the scooters and toys that the children had left lying around.

Nervously, she checked behind her, to make sure Charlie hadn't sneaked through the cat flap. Just then, a fat blackbird swooped past her nose, and she pricked up her ears in astonishment. She wasn't really used to being in the garden, and birds were new and exciting.

She swished through the long grass, almost glad now that Charlie had chased her outside. The blackbird swooped and dived in and out of the plants by the fence, and the kitten trotted after it. Then it disappeared.

Surprised, she looked around, trying to work out where it had gone. That was when she noticed the hole. There was a big gap under the fence, leading into the next-door garden. This would be a perfect way to get away from Charlie. She had been looking back every so often, to check that he wasn't following, but if she went into a different garden, he would never find her! Pleased with her plan, the kitten slipped underneath the fence, and set off to explore.

Early that Sunday morning, Amy disappeared up into her tree house, taking the book she had to read for school. It was a chilly morning for April, so she was wearing her new hoodie from Gran, and a pink fluffy scarf and hat. But even though it was cold, being up in the tree house felt wonderful.

It wasn't really all that high up, but it was such fun looking down on the gardens from her hideaway amongst the leaves. The chestnut tree was right at the end of their long, thin garden, but she could just see Mum moving around in the kitchen. Amy moved the beanbag so that it was in the doorway and flumped down on it, watching a blackbird hopping around in next-door's flower bed. There was an early morning mist hanging over the grass, and it felt quite spooky – just right for her book, which was a ghost story.

Amy read a few pages. She was just getting to a scary bit when a strange rustling noise outside made her jump. A little movement by the garden fence caught her eye, and Amy peered down. It was a little black kitten! She was half-wreathed in mist, and for a second Amy wondered if this was a ghost-cat. She caught her breath in excitement, watching as the tiny thing nosed her way through the plants and spotted the blackbird, who was still pecking about in the grass on the other side of the garden.

The kitten settled into a hunting crouch, her tail whisking from side to side, and wriggled forwards on to the lawn. Amy giggled. This was no ghost! The kitten was so funny, stalking across the grass like a tiny panther. The bird spotted her at once, hopping up on to the fence and squawking crossly.

The kitten turned away and began to play with a leaf instead, as though she'd never even thought of chasing the bird.

Amy was just wondering whether, if she climbed down quietly, the kitten would let her stroke it, when the little creature suddenly darted back the way she'd come – under the fence and into the mists of next-door's garden.

Amy watched the shadowy little figure disappear. "I wonder who she belongs to?" she whispered to herself. "And what her name is. If I could get close enough, I could look on her collar, maybe." Then she frowned. "No, I don't think she had one. I think I'd call her Misty." She put her chin in her hands, and imagined a little black kitten curled up on the end of her bed. "I can't wait to tell Lily about her!"

Chapter Three

"Have you seen her again?" Lily asked eagerly, and Amy smiled.

"Yesterday, just as I was going out into the garden. She was sitting on the back fence, right under the tree house. But when I got closer she ran off."

"You've seen her a few times now. Maybe she lives in one of the houses close by," Lily suggested.

Amy frowned. "She doesn't have a collar, though. I just wonder – perhaps she's a stray? She never comes very close – I think she's quite shy of people. A stray kitten could be like that, couldn't it?"

Lily nodded thoughtfully.

"And she looks ever so thin," Amy added. "I'm worried she isn't getting enough food."

"Poor little thing!" Lily cried. "Kittens do need to eat a lot. Or she might just be naturally skinny. Kittens can be. Oh, I wish I could see her."

"If we're lucky she might turn up when you come to tea on Friday," Amy said. Lily was a cat expert and might be able to think of a way she could help the kitten.

By now the little kitten was exploring the gardens all along the road. She had discovered that she loved being outside – there were always new and exciting things to play with. Sometimes people left food out, too. Even if it was only stale bread meant for the birds, it was better than nothing, as Charlie was still stealing most of her meals. She'd got very good at scrambling up bird tables. She wasn't as good at chasing the birds themselves – somehow they always seemed to work out that she was coming. But she enjoyed trying.

Being outside was definitely better than being at her new house, anyway. Even when Charlie left her alone, which wasn't often, Mrs Jones's two grandchildren were almost as bad. They liked to fuss over her and stroke her, which the kitten didn't mind too much. And sometimes it was quite fun to chase the string that they dangled in front of her nose. But they also kept trying to pick her up, which she hated, especially as they just grabbed her and hauled her along with her legs dangling, even though Mrs Jones had explained how to hold her properly. The kitten tried to stay out of their way.

"Puss! Puss, puss, puss! Where are you, Jet?" Millie called.

The kitten slipped quickly under the kitchen table, but it was an obvious hiding place, and the little girl crawled underneath to be with her. Jet's tail started to twitch nervously.

Millie was carrying a handful of dolls' clothes, but she dropped them on the floor and seized the kitten round her middle.

Jet yowled, wriggling desperately to get away, but the little girl held her firmly. Millie then grabbed a doll's jacket and started trying to place one of her paws into it. "You're going to look so pretty! Charlie's too big for all my dolls' clothes, but you're just the right size."

The kitten scrabbled frantically and raked her tiny claws across Millie's hand. The little girl dropped Jet in surprise, and the kitten shot out from under the table, and cowered in the corner of the kitchen, hissing furiously.

Millie howled, staring at the red scratch across the back of her hand.

"What happened?" Sarah ran into the kitchen, and Millie scrambled out from under the table. "Jet hurt me!" she wailed, holding out her hand.

"Jet did that?" Sarah turned to stare at the kitten. "Bad cat! You mustn't scratch people!" She sounded really cross, and the kitten slunk guiltily out of the kitchen to find Mrs Jones, knowing that she would understand.

Mrs Jones was in her favourite armchair as usual. But Charlie was there too. Curled up cosily on Mrs Jones's lap, looking as though he belonged there. Just where the kitten was meant to be.

Mrs Jones was dozing, and she didn't see Jet, staring wide-eyed from the corner of the room. The kitten watched for only a second, then she ran back the way she'd come, past Millie still sobbing in the kitchen, and straight out of the cat flap.

Charlie wasn't only taking her food now – he was taking Mrs Jones too.

Amy was up in the tree house, sitting by the door and looking out over the garden. She was drawing in the beautiful sketchbook that one of her aunts had given her for her birthday, with a set of new pencils too. She was trying to remember exactly what that gorgeous little kitten had looked like. She wished she had seen her closer up – she still wasn't sure exactly what colour her eyes were. She hesitated between the two greens in her new pencil box. Probably the lighter one. Smiling to herself, she finished colouring the eyes, and wrote *Misty* in the bottom corner of the page.

Every time she went up to her tree house, Amy watched out for the kitten, but she hadn't seen her for a couple of days. Maybe she had a home after all?

It was just as Amy was admitting to herself that the kitten might not come back, that she saw her again. She was walking carefully along the fence that ran across the back of Amy's garden – almost underneath the tree house. Amy caught her breath. She watched as the little creature padded along the narrow boards of the fence, like a tightrope walker. She smiled proudly to herself, noting that she had made the kitten's eyes exactly the right colour.

"Puss, puss, puss..." she called, very gently and quietly.

The kitten looked up, startled. She had been watching a white butterfly and hadn't seen the girl at all. She tensed up, ready to run. This girl was calling her like Millie had – was she going to try and pull her about, or dress her up in dolls' clothes?

But the girl didn't move. She was sitting up in a strange little house in a tree. Her voice was different too. Quieter. She didn't make the kitten feel nervous, like Dan and Millie did.

The girl moved, and the kitten stepped back a pace, wondering if she should leap down from the fence and race across the garden to safety – although she wasn't quite sure where that was, now that Mrs Jones wasn't hers any more.

But the girl didn't try to grab her. She just shifted herself so that she was perched on the ladder, her arm trailing down. The kitten looked up. If she stretched, she could just brush the girl's fingers with the side of her face. She could mark the girl with her scent. Her whiskers bristled with surprise at the idea that she might make this girl belong to her. She took a step closer, and then another, so that she could sniff the girl's fingers.

Swiftly, daringly, the kitten nudged the girl's hand. Then she leaped down from the fence and dashed back across the garden.

Chapter Four

Amy laughed delightedly to herself, as she watched the little kitten scurrying away. She could still feel the cold smudge of its nose against her hand.

"She came back!" she whispered happily to herself. She gazed down at her drawing and sighed. Misty was so much prettier in real life. Amy was sure she was a girl kitten, she was so delicate looking. Her fur was midnight-black and glossy, not the dull black of a drawing. She was very thin, though. Amy thought that she might even be thinner than when she'd seen her last week. If Misty was getting thinner, did that mean she didn't have an owner? Perhaps she'd got lost – Amy couldn't imagine anyone abandoning such a beautiful kitten. How could they?

If she was a stray… Amy played with her hair thoughtfully. She knew her mum and dad had said she was too young to look after a cat, and that if she told them she'd found a stray kitten, they would want to take it to the cat shelter. But now she had the tree house. Her own special, secret place. A perfect little house to hide a kitten in.

Amy shook her head and sighed. It was only a silly dream. But dreaming was fun…

"Guess what happened yesterday!" said Amy to Lily, as soon as their mums had said goodbye at the school gates. She grabbed her friend's hand and towed her over to a bench in a quiet corner of the playground.

"What?" Lily's eyes sparkled excitedly.

"The kitten came back again and I touched her! She came walking along our back fence when I was up in the tree house. She was really shy, but she sniffed my fingers, and sort of nudged me, you know how cats do?"

Lily nodded. "Stella does that, it's really sweet. Oh, I'm so glad I'm coming to your house tonight, maybe I'll see her too."

"The thing is, I definitely think she's got thinner since I last saw her." Amy sighed. "I'm really worried about her." She looked up at Lily. "Do you think I should feed her? I know she might belong to someone else, but I just don't see how she can. She's awfully thin."

Lily was practically bouncing up and down on the bench. "You should! You have to! But what are you going to feed her *on*?"

Amy smiled. "When you come home with me tonight, do you think you could ask to stop at the pet shop so you can buy some cat treats for Stella? I've brought some of my birthday money."

Lily nodded eagerly. "Of course. Stella really likes the salmon ones, we should get those."

Amy laughed. "I'm not sure this kitten would care about the flavour as long as it's food."

"I'll tell your mum I need a couple of extra tins of cat food, too," Lily added. "You can't just feed her on the treats."

"That would be brilliant," Amy told her gratefully.

"I can't wait to see her – can we go up in the tree house tonight and wait to see if she comes?"

Amy nodded. "I thought maybe if I put some food out, she might smell it."

"Good idea. We definitely need to get the fishy flavours then, they stink! My mum won't buy the tuna and prawn cat food, she says it makes her feel sick! A hungry kitten would smell it a mile off, I should think. Oh, Amy, this is so exciting." Lily gave her a hug. "It's almost like you're going to have your own cat after all!"

"She might not come," Amy said cautiously, but she hugged Lily back, unable to keep the smile off her face.

"You definitely want this kind!" Lily took a foil pouch of cat snacks from the shelf. "They smell really strong. The kitten won't be able to resist them." She placed the cat treats in her basket. "I've just thought, you'll have to give her a name. What are you going to call her?"

"I named her the first time I saw her," Amy admitted. "She's called Misty. Because I saw her coming towards me out of the mist, you see." She picked up a different packet of cat treats and added them to Lily's basket.

"Let's get these too – if this cat on the front was a kitten, it would look exactly like Misty."

"Very, very cute," Lily said.

"She is." Amy nodded. "I really hope she comes back this afternoon so you can see her! Oh, look, Mum's waving at us to hurry up." Amy's mum was waiting outside the pet shop for them.

"Goodness, you needed a lot of cat food!" she said to Lily, as the girls came out of the shop.

Lily giggled. "Stella is very greedy," she said, winking at Amy, or trying to; she wasn't very good at it, and had to screw up her face.

"Lily, are you all right?" Amy's mum asked. "Is there something in your eye?"

Amy burst out laughing, and her mum shook her head. "You two – sometimes I think it's a good thing I don't know what you're up to."

Amy and Lily grinned at each other. Secrets were such fun – and this was definitely the best one they had ever had.

They sneaked the cat food out into the garden while Amy's mum was preparing their tea.

"Wow!" Lily looked up at the tree house. "Your dad built that? He's brilliant!"

"It's cool, isn't it?" Amy agreed.

Lily hauled herself up the ladder and gazed around the inside of the tree house, admiring the bookshelf and the big purple beanbag.

"Come on, let's open these." Amy tore at the foil packet of cat treats eagerly. "I thought we could spread them out along the branch that almost touches the fence. I'm pretty sure Misty could jump on to it."

Amy carefully leaned out of the doorway to sprinkle some cat treats on to the wide branch below. "Now we need to wait," she said, edging backwards. She emptied the rest of the packet in the doorway just in front of her, then sat hugging her knees and staring over the gardens, searching for a little black figure.

Amy and Lily had meant to be totally silent, so as not to scare away the kitten, but they couldn't resist chatting. They were deep in a discussion of exactly why Luke Armstrong in Mrs Dale's class was so mean, when Amy suddenly clutched Lily's arm.

"Look!" she ordered, in a hissing whisper.

"Oh!" Lily gave a little squeak of excitement. "Is that her?"

"I think so." Amy leaned out to look further along the fence, where a black shadow was clambering over the ivy branches. "Yes, it's her! Oh, I hope she can smell the cat biscuits."

Scrambling through the leaves, her paws slipping on the thin branches, the kitten certainly could. She was terribly hungry. Charlie was still stealing all her food, and no one seemed to notice – Sarah was always busy, and Mrs Jones wasn't very well and was spending most of her time resting in her chair. Quite often she had Charlie sitting on her now, and she would stroke him, while the kitten watched miserably from under the sofa, or peeping out from under the bookcase.

But now she could smell something tangy and lovely, and her stomach was making little rumbling noises. She trotted eagerly along the fence.

Oh, the smell was getting even stronger and better.

The kitten stopped suddenly, and wobbled on the fence. She was there – the girl from yesterday! And there was another one with her. The kitten watched them warily.

Then the girl she'd seen before held out a little packet, and tipped something out of it, and the kitten knew that was where the wonderful smell was coming from. The tip of her little pink tongue stuck out, she was so hungry.

Amy couldn't help giggling. The kitten was so cute, with her tongue just poking out like that. It made her look really silly.

The kitten put her front paws up on the tree branch, and the girls exchanged excited glances. Then she jumped all the way up, and found the first cat treat. She crunched it up in seconds, and scampered forwards, sniffing for more. When she got to the end of the branch, after about six more treats, she stopped and looked anxiously at Amy and Lily. She could see – and smell – the big pile of treats just in front of them.

Amy sighed. "Perhaps she's too frightened to come closer," she whispered.

Suddenly, the kitten sprung up on to

the tree house ladder, and Amy and Lily held their breath. Then, keeping one eye on the girls, she started to gobble up the treats from the doorway.

When they were all gone, she licked the place where they'd been, then looked up hopefully.

"She's still hungry!" Amy said. "Let's open another packet."

Lily shook her head. "No way. She'll be sick. A whole packet's loads more than she should have, anyway!"

Amy nodded. Then she held out one hand, very slowly, to the kitten, who was staring at her seriously. Amy scratched her gently behind the ears, and she half-closed her eyes with pleasure.

"Hello, Misty," Amy whispered.

Chapter Five

The kitten sat there a little nervously, still ready to run, as Amy stroked her and then Lily joined in too.

"Isn't she beautiful?" Amy said proudly.

"The prettiest kitten I've ever seen – except Stella," Lily added, out of loyalty. "Oh, Amy, she's started purring!"

She had. Amy had just found the exact itchy spot behind her left ear, and the kitten had her eyes closed, and a tiny little throaty purr was making Amy's hand buzz.

"Tea, girls!"

The kitten's eyes shot open. She leaped off the ladder and raced back along the branch, jumping down on to the fence and disappearing away.

"Bye, Misty!" Amy called after her quietly. "Why did Mum have to pick just then to call?" she complained to Lily, as they scrambled down from the tree house. "I think Misty might even have let us pick her up."

Lily nodded. "She was definitely friendly. But you're right, she is much too thin. When I stroked her I could feel her ribs. She needs a nice owner to feed her properly."

The kitten obviously agreed. She came back to the tree house the next afternoon at the same time, and Amy opened one of the tins of cat food she'd bought. She put it in an old plastic bowl she'd borrowed from the kitchen cupboard, and sat in the doorway of the tree house, watching Misty gobble it down. Misty let Amy stroke her again, too, and even put her paws on Amy's leg, as though she was considering climbing into her lap.

"Are you going out to the tree house again?" Mum asked. "It's raining, though! I didn't realize you loved it that much."

"It's my best present ever!" Amy giggled, a little guiltily. She *did* love the tree house, but that wasn't the main reason she was spending so much time out there. Every afternoon that week, as soon as she got home, she'd rushed straight there to look out for Misty.

She threw on her hoodie over her uniform and went out to the tree house. The ladder was slippery from the rain so she climbed up slowly, peering out along the fence for a little kitten. But no kitten came running to see her today. She sighed. Maybe Misty was sheltering from the rain somewhere.

She stood up and pulled open the tree house door, planning to sit and read on the beanbag, while keeping an eye out for Misty through the window.

But the beanbag was already occupied.

A little kitten – her fur shiny and spiky from the rain – was curled up on it, fast asleep.

Now that she had discovered that the tree house had a soft, comfortable place to sleep, and that Amy would come and feed her, Misty spent most of her days there, even though she still went back to Mrs Jones to sleep at night. She had climbed in through the half-open window that first time to get out of the rain, and Amy hadn't seemed to mind. In fact, she'd looked really pleased, and spent ages stroking her. The window was always open a little way now, so that she could get in, and there would always be a little bowl of cat crunchies or something else delicious waiting for her.

"I don't know if I'm imagining it, but I think you're looking plumper," Amy told the kitten lovingly, a week after she'd first found her inside the tree house. She stroked the little black tummy, as the kitten lay sleepily in her lap. "Are you getting fatter, Misty?"

"Prrrrp." The kitten purred, and yawned. Then she snuggled up on Amy's lap, feeling more at home than she had for a long time.

Amy stroked her gently, wishing Misty was really hers. "Stay here, puss," she murmured. "This is your tree house now too." But it was getting dark now and Amy knew she'd have to head inside soon, and leave the kitten all alone.

"Amy! Your tea's getting cold!" came her mum's voice, from just below the tree house.

Amy jumped and so did Misty, springing off her lap.

She could hear her mum climbing up the ladder. Panicking, Amy dropped her hoodie top over Misty. She couldn't let the secret out now – not when Misty felt almost hers. Mum would never let her keep a kitten.

Amy's mum poked her head through the doorway. "I've been calling you for ages!"

"Sorry!" Amy got up quickly and went over to her mum, hoping she wouldn't see the wriggling hoodie behind her. She followed her down the ladder.

Misty edged her way out from under the top, shaking her fur crossly. Why had Amy done that?

She slunk over to the tree house door and watched Amy going up the garden towards the house. Misty slipped out along the branch, and jumped down on to the fence, then into Amy's garden. Keeping her distance, she followed Amy, trotting after her. But just as she reached the house, Amy closed the door.

Misty stood outside it sadly. She wished she could follow Amy into the house. It looked warm and friendly.

There was a big magnolia tree, growing close to the kitchen window, and Misty scrambled up the trunk to a branch, then jumped on to the window sill. She could see Amy, and two other people, laughing and eating.

The food smelled delicious. She mewed, hoping that Amy would see her and let her in. But the man sitting closest to the window was the one who stood up and came to look.

"It's a cat!" He laughed. "A little black kitten. Come and see, Amy."

Amy jumped as she saw Misty, accidentally knocking her glass of juice off the table. It smashed on the floor, and the woman got up with a sigh.

Misty leaped back on to the branch, hiding in the gathering darkness, and watching as they cleared up the mess. She wished she was in there with them, but Amy had seemed upset to see her and she didn't know why. Misty watched for a while, until Amy disappeared and the lights went off. Then she pattered sadly down the garden and back up into the tree house. But this time she didn't sleep on the beanbag. She curled up on the hoodie top instead. It smelled of Amy.

"Mum came up to the tree house and nearly saw Misty last night!" Amy told Lily before school on Friday morning. "I had to throw my hoodie on top of her, poor thing! And then she was suddenly there at the window, and Dad saw her!" She sighed. "It's fun having a secret kitten, but I wish I didn't have to hide her all the time. It would be so nice to be able to take her inside, too. I'd love her to sleep on my bed, like Stella does with you."

"It is nice," Lily admitted. "She keeps my toes toasty. Do you think your mum and dad really wouldn't let you keep her?"

Amy shook her head thoughtfully. "I just don't know. I've begged for a kitten for so long – if they were going to let me have one, wouldn't they have given in by now? I can't see them changing their minds."

"But she's so cute!"

"Maybe I should tell them all about Misty. But what if they make me take her to a cat shelter?" Amy shuddered at the thought.

Even so, she couldn't stop imagining how lovely it would be to curl up and sleep with her own little kitten. She just had to think of a way…

"This is brilliant!" Lily said excitedly, as she laid out her sleeping bag on the floor of the tree house. "I'm so glad Mum agreed I could stay over. Do you really think Misty will come and sleep with us too?"

"I think she spends the night here sometimes now. I tried brushing all the cat hairs off the beanbag last night, and there were more this morning. So she must have been here…"

Amy had come up with the sleepover plan at school, and the girls had begged their mums to let them do it that Saturday. Lily's mum had been a bit worried that they would be cold, but she'd agreed in the end, when Lily reminded her about the special sleeping bags they'd bought to go camping. She even had a spare one for Amy!

"This is even better than camping! Oh, I do hope Misty comes," Lily said excitedly, as she clambered into her sleeping bag.

Amy nodded, glancing over at the window from her sleeping bag. It was too dark to see much – especially a black kitten. Misty had spent the afternoon in the tree house, but she'd run off when Amy started to move things around to get ready for the sleepover.

They chatted for ages by the light of their torches, but they kept yawning as it grew later and later.

"I don't think she's going to come," Amy said sadly, when she looked at her watch and discovered it was ten o'clock.

"Never mind." Lily gave her a hug. "It's a brilliant sleepover anyway. Maybe we'll see her in the morning."

Amy nodded, but she did feel disappointed. And as Lily yawned more and more, and then drifted off to sleep, she felt lonely too. The wind was blowing and she could hear the creak of the branches. It seemed to shake the tree house more at night, although she didn't see why it would. Amy lay there with her torch making a circle on the ceiling, worrying about Misty.

Where was she on this chilly night?
Was someone looking after her?

A sudden thud made her yelp with
fright, and she swung her torch round.
The beam caught a pair of glowing
green eyes, staring at her in surprise.

"Misty! You came!"

Purring delightedly, the kitten raced across the boards to leap on to Amy's sleeping bag, padding at it eagerly with her determined little paws.

Amy lay down again, and yawned. "I'm so glad you're here," she murmured.

Misty curled up next to Amy's shoulder, half inside the sleeping bag. It was wonderfully warm. She was very glad she was there, too.

Amy stroked Misty gently, and soon the pair of them were fast asleep.

Chapter Six

"Oh, Amy, she's here!"

Amy blinked sleepily, and looked over at Lily, who was sitting up in her sleeping bag. There was a warm, furry weight on her chest, and Amy remembered her late night visitor. Misty had stayed all night!

"She turned up a little while after you went to sleep." Amy suddenly sat up, making Misty squeak. "Lily, what time is it? My mum! She said she'd bring us our breakfast in the morning."

Lily's eyes widened. "It feels like we slept quite late." She wriggled over to the door and opened it. "Oh no, she's coming down the garden! With toast!"

"I don't care if she's got toast! What are we going to do?"

But they were both sleepy and giggly with excitement about Misty, and all Amy could think of was to pull her sleeping bag up over the kitten. Which Misty didn't like. She wriggled about indignantly, and just as Amy's mum appeared at the top of the ladder, she poked her head back out.

"Hello, girls! Did you sleep well?"
Amy's mum smiled at them. "I thought
you might be hungry." Then she
noticed Misty, and her eyes widened.
"Amy, is that a cat?"

"It's a kitten," Amy told her,
cuddling Misty close.

"Where on earth has it come from?" her mother asked, sounding confused.

"I found her," Amy said defensively. "She's a stray. I've been looking after her."

"But she must belong to someone. Oh, Amy, I think we need to speak to your dad about this. Come back to the house, right now."

Amy climbed awkwardly down the ladder, with Misty still snuggled up against her pyjamas. Misty was shivering, as if she could tell that something was wrong.

Amy's dad was drinking some tea at the table, and looked up in surprise as he spotted Amy holding Misty.

"Amy, isn't that the kitten who was at the window the other day?" he said, getting up to take a closer look.

Misty hissed nervously, as this big man suddenly loomed over her.

"Sorry, kitty. I didn't mean to scare you. She's a sweet little thing, isn't she?"

"But whose sweet little thing, that's the point!" Amy's mum said.

"I don't think Misty belongs to anyone, Mrs Griffiths," Lily put in.

"She's got a name? Amy, you've named her?" Amy's mum stared at them suspiciously. "This isn't just a one-off thing, is it? How long have you been keeping this kitten in your tree house?"

"I haven't been keeping her there. She just came! I first saw her a couple of weeks ago. Just after my birthday. But I don't know how often she sleeps there."

Mum turned to Lily. "All that cat food that you bought! Was that for this kitten?" she demanded.

"Ye-es," Lily admitted, looking guilty.

Mum sighed. "Amy, it's not up to you to feed somebody else's cat! We'll never get rid of her now. Not if you've been feeding her. We need to find the kitten's owner."

"She doesn't have an owner!" Amy protested.

"She must do," her mum said firmly.

"Honestly, she doesn't. She's a stray. She really doesn't belong to anyone. She doesn't even have a collar. And look how thin she is!" Amy paused and looked at Misty. "Well, she isn't now, but that's only because I've been feeding her. She was so skinny, Mum! Ask Lily."

Amy's mum sank down into a chair. "I know you two are in this together," she snapped. "I can't believe you've both been hiding someone else's kitten!"

"Sorry, Mrs Griffiths..." Lily muttered, and Amy put an arm round her, feeling upset. She hadn't meant to get her friend into trouble.

Amy's dad pulled up a chair and took a sip of his tea. "OK. Let's not get upset," he said. "Sit down, girls, and tell us what happened with the kitten."

Amy sat down next to her dad. She looked up at Mum, determined to make her understand. "Misty was really nervous at first. It took ages before she'd let me pick her up. She was really scared. Even if she did have an owner, they haven't looked after her properly."

Misty put her paws on the table, and sniffed hopefully at Dad's tea.

Dad laughed. "She looks hungry.

Shall I give her some milk? Since Amy's already been feeding her, it can't make that much difference."

Amy's mum only sighed, but Amy shook her head. "No, Dad. Cats aren't supposed to drink milk. It gives them a stomach upset. You can give her some water, though. And I could go and get one of her tins from the tree house, if you like?"

Misty mewed hopefully, and Amy's dad nodded. "She knows what you just said. Go on then."

When Amy and Lily came back, Misty was sitting on her dad's lap.

"Dad! I didn't know you liked cats!"

"She was pretty determined." He shrugged. But he was smiling, and he stroked Misty's head very gently, as though he knew exactly how to handle a kitten.

Amy watched, wide-eyed. Mum and Dad had always been so firm about her not having a cat that she'd thought they didn't like them. But Dad looked really happy having Misty on his knee. Amy stared at him hopefully, and then exchanged a thoughtful look with Lily.

Just then, Misty jumped lightly off Amy's dad's lap, stepped delicately around the table to her mum, and sat staring pleadingly up at her, her sparkling green eyes looking as big as saucers.

"She's a charmer!" Amy's dad laughed. "She wants to stay."

"Stay! We can't keep her! I can't believe you're giving in!" Amy's mum protested. "Yes, she is cute, but we said Amy was too young for a pet."

"She's been looking after this one quite well so far," Amy's dad pointed out. "I didn't know cats shouldn't have milk. And this is a very sweet little cat." Misty mewed hopefully at Amy's mum.

"We'd better feed her, anyway," Mum said, shaking her head. "She's obviously hungry."

Amy lifted Misty down from the table and placed her on the floor, while her mum took down an old bowl. Mum opened the tin of cat food and started to empty it out. Purring, Misty butted her head against her leg, making Mum laugh with surprise.

Mum shook her head. "I never thought I'd say this, but all right.

You can keep her here – for the moment. If we find out she actually belongs to someone else, she goes straight back! And I'm going to ring the vet, and check no one's asked about a lost kitten. All right?"

Amy threw her arms around her mum. "Yes. But she doesn't have an owner, I'm sure." She then looked down at the kitten, who was tucking into the food greedily. "This is your new home, Misty!"

Chapter Seven

Over the next few days, even Amy's mum got used to the idea of having a cat. Misty was so sweet, and very well-behaved. Amy's mum had been worried about her making messes in the house, but Amy's dad went out and bought a litter tray, and Misty soon showed that she was beautifully house trained.

"I don't think she can have been born feral," Amy's mum said, tickling Misty under the chin. "She's so friendly. I'm still worried she's somebody's pet."

Amy folded her arms and frowned. "Well, it was somebody who didn't love her as much as we do!" She sighed. "OK, OK, Mum. I promise. We'll give her back, if anyone says they've lost her." But she was certain they wouldn't.

Misty and Amy still spent a lot of time in the tree house. It was Misty's favourite place, and Amy loved curling up there with her. But once Misty had proved she could use the litter tray, she was allowed anywhere in the house, too. She loved exploring – the house was full of warm, comfortable places.

And Amy's dad was very good to sit on. She was even allowed to sleep on Amy's bed, since she hated being shut in the kitchen. They had tried it on her first night in the house, but Misty had mewed frantically, and in the end Amy's mum had given in. Now she slept snuggled up with Amy, or sometimes blissfully curled on Amy's toes.

Amy spent the last of her birthday money buying her toys, and a collar – a pink one that looked beautiful against her black fur.

Misty could still remember her old home with Mrs Jones, but she knew she belonged to Amy now.

Mrs Jones sat in her armchair, staring out at the front garden, and stroking Charlie. But she was frowning. "It's been a week since I've seen Jet now," she murmured to the Siamese cat. "I hadn't realized, because she was only popping in and out even before. But she hasn't even been back for her food." She looked down at Charlie, worriedly. "I have to say, Charlie, you're a bit heavier than you used to be. Have you been eating Jet's meals?" She pushed him gently off her lap, and stood up, leaning on her stick. Slowly, she walked into the kitchen, with Charlie trotting after her.

"Sarah, when did you last see Jet?" said Mrs Jones, easing herself on to a kitchen chair.

Her daughter looked surprised. "Oh. I don't know, Mum." She glanced over at the cat food bowls, both of which were empty. "Well, she's eaten her breakfast, so she must have been here this morning, although I didn't actually see her." She smiled as Charlie wove around her ankles. "It's a pity we can't ask him!"

"Hmm." Mrs Jones frowned. "I don't think we need to ask him. It's clear exactly who's been eating Jet's food. Look how much plumper he is!"

Sarah shook her head. "Oh no. He wouldn't!"

"Sarah, I haven't seen Jet for a week. And before then she was so flighty and scared that I'd only see her here and there for a second. I think Charlie frightened her away."

"Charlie's not like that, really…" But Sarah was looking a little worried.

"It isn't his fault," said Mrs Jones. "This is his house, after all. But we have to find Jet. I should've realized what was going on, but those new pills Dr Jackson gave me made me so tired. Poor Jet! She must be starving by now.

She doesn't know the area at all… She might've got lost or she could even have been run over." Mrs Jones's voice wobbled at the thought.

Sarah came over and put her arm comfortingly around her mother. "Don't worry, Mum, we'll find Jet. I'm sure she can't have gone far."

One afternoon, a fortnight after their sleepover, Amy and Lily were walking back from school, chatting away as their mums followed behind.

"Dad's going to put in a cat flap this weekend," Amy told her friend happily.

But Lily didn't reply. Amy looked round and realized that Lily wasn't actually there. She'd stopped and was looking up at something stuck to the lamp post they'd just passed.

Amy went back to see what Lily was staring at. "What is it? Oh no…"

It was a poster, with a photo of a small kitten, and the words: "LOST. Jet, a black kitten. Please check sheds and garages in case she has been trapped inside. Contact Mrs Sylvia Jones if you have seen our cat." Underneath there was a phone number and an address.

Amy stared at the poster numbly. "Do you – do you think it's Misty?" she whispered to Lily.

"It looks ever so like her," Lily admitted sadly. "And Rose Tree Close is only round the corner from you, isn't it?"

Tears welled up in Amy's eyes. "I don't want to give her back," she muttered. "It isn't fair. Misty doesn't love this Mrs Jones, whoever she is. She can't do, or she wouldn't have come to live with us. And think how thin Misty was when we first saw her – she mustn't have looked after her properly!"

LOST KITTEN

Lily nodded. "What are you going to do?"

Amy looked up at the poster. "I could just pretend I haven't seen it. That Mrs Jones doesn't deserve to have Misty back – I wouldn't feel guilty." Then she gazed at the photo of Misty again. "Well, only a little bit…"

She glanced along the road. Her mum and Lily's had nearly caught them up. She could just tear down the poster, then Mum would never know… But as her mum approached Amy could see that she was holding another copy that she must have taken from somewhere further down the street.

"Oh, Amy. You've seen it too. I'm so sorry, but it looks like Misty has a home after all."

"But how do we know it's her?" Amy whispered.

"She does look very similar," Mum said gently.

"She didn't like her old home, or she wouldn't have run away. She's ours now. Dad was even going to put in a cat flap!"

"I know, Amy. But someone's missing her – this Mrs Jones—"

"She doesn't deserve a kitten!" Amy sniffed, and Lily squeezed her hand.

"We have to take her back," said Mum. "Remember, it was our deal."

Amy was silent for a moment. There was nothing she could say. "I know. But I still think it's wrong."

Back home, Misty wasn't in the house, running to the door with welcoming mews, like she usually did.

"Maybe she's in the tree house," Amy suggested. But a little seed of hope was growing inside her. If she couldn't find Misty, she wouldn't have to give her back, would she?

Amy ran out into the garden, and climbed up to the tree house, but it was empty. She sat down on the beanbag. It felt warm, as though Misty might have been curled up there until a moment ago. "Oh, Misty, I wish I'd kept you a secret," she whispered. "Please don't come!"

But then she heard a familiar thud on the boards of the tree house, as Misty jumped from the branch. The tears spilled down Amy's cheeks, as the kitten ran to her, leaping into her lap.

Misty rubbed her head lovingly

against Amy's arm, and then stood up with her paws on Amy's shoulder, and licked the wet tear trails with her rough little tongue.

"That tickles!" Amy half-laughed, half-sobbed. She picked her up gently. "Sorry, Misty, we have to go and find Mum." Amy carried her down from the tree house and across the garden. Misty purred in her arms, so happily. She was such a different kitten from the nervous little creature Amy had first seen. It felt so wrong to take her back!

"Oh, you found her!" Mum came over to stroke Misty, as Amy opened the kitchen door. "Please don't cry, Amy." But she looked close to crying herself, as she gave Amy a hug. "I don't want to give her back either, but we have to. You know we do. Look, shall we wait until tomorrow? So you can have tonight to say goodbye?"

Amy shook her head. "No. That would be worse. We should go now. Come on, Mum, please, let's just get it over with."

"All right. I'll call the number on the poster. Rose Tree Close isn't far. We can just carry her there, can't we?"

Amy nodded, and sat down at the table with Misty, half-listening as Mum explained to someone on the phone that they'd found their missing kitten. With shaking fingers, Amy started to take off Misty's pink collar. Misty wasn't even Misty any more! She had another name.

"They're really glad to know she's safe," Mum told her gently. "I said we'd bring her round." She grabbed her bag, and they set out, Amy with Misty held tightly in her arms as they walked down their street and along another road, to the little turning that was Rose Tree Close.

Misty looked around her curiously, wondering what was happening. Amy had never carried her outside like this before. Then, all of a sudden, her ears went back flat against her head, as she recognized where they were going.

Why was Amy bringing her *here*? She struggled in Amy's arms and mewed with fright as they walked down the path.

"Oh, Mum, she doesn't want to!" Amy protested, but her mum had already rung the doorbell.

The door opened, and an old lady stood there, staring at them in delight.

"Jet! It really is her! Oh, thank you so much for finding her!"

Amy only just stopped herself from shouting, "No, her name's Misty!" Instead, she stared at the brooch on the old lady's cardigan, which was a little silver cat, with green glass eyes.

"Come in, please! Oh, Jet, where have you been?" Mrs Jones stroked Misty, and Misty actually relaxed and purred, and let the old lady take her from Amy.

Amy felt the tears starting to burn the backs of her eyes again. This really was Misty's owner. It was true. Her little cat belonged to someone else.

Chapter Eight

Misty felt very confused. She was back with Mrs Jones, but Amy was there too. She wasn't sure what was happening. Mrs Jones had Charlie now, so why had Amy brought her here? But it was so nice to have Mrs Jones holding her again. She rubbed herself against the old lady's cheek lovingly.

Mrs Jones led them into the sitting

room, and sat down with Misty on her lap. "Where did you find her?" she asked, smiling at them so gratefully that Amy felt guilty.

"She came into Amy's tree house," her mum explained. "We did ask around, but no one seemed to have lost a kitten. She's actually been with us a couple of weeks. I'm sorry, you must have been so worried."

Mrs Jones nodded. "I was terrified that she'd got lost or had even been run over. I've only just moved here, you see, to live with my daughter, so Jet doesn't know the area very well." She scratched Misty behind the ears, and the little cat stretched her paws out blissfully. "She kept wandering off – we hardly saw her – and then she disappeared. I thought she'd gone too far and got lost."

Mum gave Amy a look, and Amy stared at the carpet, feeling miserable and guilty. Mrs Jones had hardly seen her because Amy had been tempting her away. She'd been so stupid! Mum had been right – she really had stolen someone else's cat.

"Amy looked after her very well," her mum said, giving Amy a hug. "We'd always thought she was too young for a pet, but we've changed our minds after watching her with your cat. We're definitely going to get a kitten of our own. I mean it," she added to Amy in a whisper. "We're so proud of you."

There was a scuffling noise at the door, and Misty suddenly tensed up. She had forgotten! It had been beautifully quiet, almost like things used to be, with just Mrs Jones. But now Millie and Dan were home!

"Gran! Gran! Oh! You've got Jet back!" A little boy raced into the room, and tried to grab Misty.

Amy gasped, as she watched Misty cower back against Mrs Jones. A little girl came running in after him, and tried to pull her brother away so she could reach the kitten too.

"Gently, Dan! Millie, be careful! You'll frighten her," Mrs Jones cried. The children stopped shoving as their mum came in. "These are my grandchildren. They've missed her too," Mrs Jones explained to Amy and her mum. "And this is my daughter, Sarah."

Sarah was smiling delightedly. "I'm so glad you've found her. We've all been so worried."

Amy looked anxiously at Misty – or Jet, she supposed she ought to call her now. She was pressed against Mrs Jones, her ears twitching with fright. Amy thought the children were loud, so she couldn't imagine how a kitten felt.

"We'd better go – leave you all to settle down," Amy's mum said.

"Please, let me have your number – I'd like to call and let you know how Jet is. I'm really so grateful." Mrs Jones stood up, with Jet held against her shoulder, and led them out into the hallway. "My goodness! Jet, what is it?"

The kitten suddenly scrabbled her way up Mrs Jones's shoulder, and leaped to the top of a shelf, almost knocking over a vase. Her tail was fluffed up, and her ears were laid back. Charlie was here!

"Oh, you've got another cat!" Amy exclaimed, seeing the sleek Siamese padding along the hallway, staring up at her little Misty.

"Yes, that's Charlie. He belongs to my daughter. He and Jet don't always get along too well. But I'm sure they'll settle down now that she's back."

Watching Misty spitting angrily from her safe spot on the shelf, Amy thought that it didn't look like they got along at all.

"You were very good, Amy," her mum said, as they walked home. "I really did mean it about you getting your own kitten."

"Thanks," Amy whispered. "Not for a while though," she added. She knew she ought to be happy at the idea of her own kitten. But at the moment all she could think of was Misty, scared by those noisy, grabby children, and terrified of that Siamese cat. It made her want to cry. When she'd first seen Misty with Mrs Jones, she'd thought she'd got it all wrong, and Misty did belong with her. But now she wasn't sure. What if that Siamese had been stealing all of Misty's food and that's how the kitten had ended up so thin? She wouldn't be surprised. She was almost sure that Charlie had made Misty run away. And now Amy had made her go back.

Misty raced across the living room, making for her hiding place under the bookshelf. But she couldn't get in! She wriggled frantically, but she'd grown – two weeks of proper food, and she was simply too big to fit into her special safe place. Why had Amy left her here? Was she going to come back? Shaking, she turned back to face Charlie, who was right on her tail. She hissed defiantly, and raked her little claws across his nose. But he was just so big! With one swipe of his long brown paw he sent her rolling over and over across the carpet, and then he jumped on her.

"Honestly! Mum, she's fighting with Charlie already! Stop it! Bad cat!" Sarah tried to pull the two of them apart as they scratched and spat.

Mrs Jones heaved herself up from her chair, and tried to help. "Jet, Jet, come here. Oh, he's hurting her." She waved Charlie away with her walking stick, and leaned down to scoop up the little kitten. "Oh dear..." She sat down again, the kitten a ball of trembling black fur in her arms.

"Charlie hates not being able to use the cat flap, that's why he's being grumpy," Sarah muttered, picking up

Charlie, and holding him as he wriggled and spat at Jet.

"I know, but Jet might run off again, if we let her out. We need to keep her in for now, so she starts thinking of this as her home." Mrs Jones stroked her gently.

Sarah sighed. "We'll just have to keep them apart until they get used to each other."

Mrs Jones looked worriedly down at the kitten, still shaking on her lap.

"Maybe I was wrong to say you'd get along with Charlie… I suppose I was just so pleased to have you back. Poor little Jet. Whatever are we going to do with you two?"

After school a few days later, Amy was up in the tree house lying with her head resting on the beanbag. There were little black hairs on it here and there. She looked up and saw that, sitting on the shelf, there was still one tin of cat food left, that she'd never remembered to bring into the house. It was all she had left of Misty, that and her collar, which was on her bedside table.

Mum kept mentioning the idea of

another kitten, and Lily had bought her a cat magazine, so she could look at what sort of cat she might like. But Amy just couldn't think about it yet. It would feel like betraying Misty – betraying her all over again, because Amy felt sure they had done the wrong thing by taking Misty home. She kept listening out for that telltale thump on the wooden boards that meant Misty was coming back to her, but it never came. She supposed Mrs Jones was keeping Misty shut up so she didn't stray again.

It had been five days. Nearly a week. Perhaps after a week, they'd let Misty go out into the garden? Maybe she'd come walking along the fence again, and Amy could at least stroke her.

That wouldn't do any harm, would it? As long as Amy didn't feed her, no one could say she was trying to tempt her back. Even just seeing her would be enough. All she wanted was to know that Misty was all right.

Mum was calling her for tea. Amy looked hopefully along the fence as she climbed down the ladder, but there was no Misty trotting along to see her.

She sat down at the kitchen table, picking at her pasta and staring at the newspaper ad that Mum had ringed. "Kittens, eight weeks old. Tabby and white." Amy didn't want a tabby and white cat. She wanted a black one. A very particular black one.

"Has Charlie finished his dinner, Sarah? Can we let Jet in?" Mrs Jones was peering round the kitchen door, with Jet in her arms.

Charlie looked up at her and hissed crossly. He hadn't finished, and he didn't want that kitten anywhere near his food.

"Oh, Charlie," Sarah sighed. "They really aren't getting on any better, are they?"

Mrs Jones shook her head. "I'm beginning to wonder if I did the right thing," she admitted, her voice sad. "Maybe I should have let that little girl keep her. You could see she was heartbroken when she brought Jet back."

"But you'd miss her!" Sarah protested.

"Of course I would! But I think she'd be well looked after. And we still have Charlie. He's a lovely boy, he just doesn't like sharing his house…"

Sarah nodded. "Oh, he's finished." She picked up Charlie, and took him over to the door to put him out.

Misty watched as Sarah began to open the door, and her whiskers trembled with sudden excitement. The garden! The fence! And along the fence, just waiting for her, was Amy's garden, and Amy's house, and Amy.

She wriggled frantically, and made the most enormous leap out of Mrs Jones's arms. She shot out of the door before Sarah could even think to shut it.

She was going home.

Amy sighed, and stared down at her homework. She was supposed to be writing about her favourite place, but the only place she could think of was the tree house, with Misty curled up on the beanbag. A sudden scuffling at the kitchen window made her look up.

"Misty!" Dad exclaimed, looking up from the pan he was stirring on the hob.

Amy ran to the door to let her in. She knelt down and swept Misty up into her arms. Misty purred gleefully, rubbing her face against Amy's.

Amy was laughing, and half-crying at the same time. "She came back," she murmured, and Misty licked her hand gently. Amy's dad tickled Misty under the chin, then her mum came over to stroke her, too.

"Mum, do we have to...?" Amy asked miserably. "She's so happy to be here..." She looked pleadingly over at her dad, but he shook his head sadly.

Her mum sighed. "I know. I wish we could just keep her, but it wouldn't be fair. She doesn't belong to us." She picked up the phone.

"Mrs Jones? It's Emily Griffiths here. Yes, I'm afraid we've got Misty again. Sorry, I mean Jet."

Amy sat down on one of the kitchen chairs, and stroked Misty as she watched her mum miserably.

Her dad put a comforting hand on her shoulder. Maybe Mrs Jones was going out, Amy thought. Maybe it wouldn't be a good time to bring Misty back, and they could keep her for just one night. But that would be worse, wouldn't it? She'd never be able to give her up then.

Misty wriggled indignantly as a tear fell on her head, and then another.

"Really?" The note of surprise in her mum's voice made Amy look up. "Well, if you're sure. We'd be delighted."

Amy stared at her, sudden hope making her feel almost sick. She watched her mother put down the phone and turn around, beaming. "That was the first time Misty had been out, Amy. She came straight back to you. Mrs Jones says that she obviously thinks she's your cat now, and it isn't fair to keep her. She's given Misty to you." She hugged them all – Amy and Misty and Dad together. "Well, we promised you a kitten, didn't we?"

"Oh, Mum! Wait a minute." Amy pressed Misty gently into her dad's arms, and dashed upstairs, then raced back down again and into the kitchen, with something pink in her hand.

Carefully, she fastened Misty's collar back on. "You're really ours now. You're here to stay," Amy murmured, taking the kitten from Dad.

Snuggling against Amy's neck, Misty closed her eyes and purred – a tiny, happy noise. She was home!

Photo copyright © Nigel Bird

Holly Webb started out as a children's book editor, and wrote her first series for the publisher she worked for. She has been writing ever since, with over sixty books to her name. Holly lives in Berkshire, with her husband and three young sons. She has two pet cats called Milly and Marble, who are always nosying around when Holly is trying to type on her laptop.